CREATION STORIES

IN FOLK TALES FROM AROUND THE WORLD

RETOLD BY FIONA WATERS

ILLUSTRATED BY LIZ PYLE

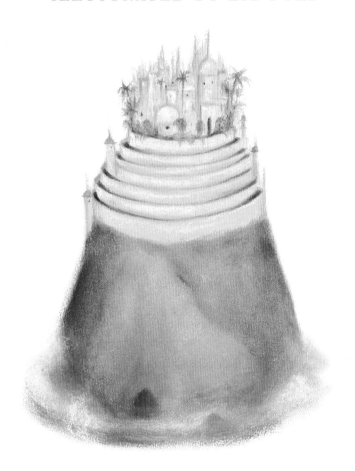

Belitha Press

First published in the UK in 2002 by

Belitha Press Ltd
A member of **Chrysalis** Books plc
64 Brewery Road
London N7 9NT

ISBN 1 84138 319 8

British Library Cataloguing in Publication Data for
this book is available from the British Library.

Editor: Russell Mclean
Series editor: Mary-Jane Wilkins
Designer: Sarah Goodwin
Illustrator: Liz Pyle

Printed in Taiwan

10 9 8 7 6 5 4 3 2 1

CONTENTS

For Juliet with much love - F.W.

For George and
Ned with love - L.P.

THE CREATION OF THE EARTH

LONG, LONG BEFORE there was anything in the universe there was nothing. Everywhere was very dark, complete and utter dark. A dark mass of nothing, utter chaos. Nothingness. In the midst of the nothingness, of all things, there floated an egg. A huge great egg. Of course this was no ordinary egg. Inside the egg were dark and light, wet and dry, cold and heat, the heavy yolk and the light white – all that was needed to create the earth, Yin and Yang. But also in the egg was P'an-ku, the first ever living being. The egg floated in the nothingness for eighteen thousand years.

And all the while the egg floated through the dark of every day. For eighteen thousand years P'an-ku grew. Oh, so slowly, slowly he grew. He grew tall and heavy. His hair grew long and tangled. His nails lengthened and curled. His great knees and elbows grew bony and sharp, and they pressed against the sides of the eggshell. And as time passed the great P'an-ku grew too large for his egg. With a sharp crack, the shell broke in two.

P'an-ku was free. As he stretched, the top and bottom of the eggshell separated. The light top half clung to P'an-ku's shaggy head as he achingly rose to his feet, and it formed the sky. The heavy bottom half sank down and lay under his huge feet, and it became the earth.

So great was P'an-ku's strength that he pushed the sky and the earth further and further apart until he stood like a great pillar between the two. And so the sky and the earth were in their rightful places. Every day the earth grew deeper by another ten feet, and the sky loftier by another ten feet.

P'an-ku held the sky and the earth apart, the sky on his shoulders and the earth firmly under his feet, for thousands of years more until his hair grew white, his skin wrinkled and his strength waned. And then, as P'an-ku's body crumbled,

the great world took shape. His huge head became vast mountain ranges, their peaks lost in the height of the sky. His teeth tumbled to the ground as mighty boulders. His right eye gleamed in the sky as the hot sun, his left hid and only came out as the moon when the sun had disappeared. His arms and legs formed the north and south, the east and west of the new world. His flesh and bones made the soil, his white billowing hair the trees and plants. And the earth was built around the fragments of his body, marking the five points of the Chinese compass.

His tears made the rain and as it fell it ran into the mighty rivers, lakes and seas that had been formed by his blood. His breath made the winds that blew from all four corners of the new earth, and his voice was the low rumble of thunder.

When P'an-ku was happy the sun shone and the skies were blue, but when he was angry the clouds rolled in, dark and brooding, and the winds blew up a storm.

Last of all, the tiny fleas that hopped around his body tumbled down and became the people and animals that walked the earth. He gave the people his own ancient but simple wisdom and they lived in harmony for a very long time. The first four special beasts were a dragon, a tortoise, a phoenix and a unicorn, and they walked the earth, filling the forests and seas, the mountainsides and the caves. And thus it was that the wondrous earth and glorious heavens were created by P'an-ku.

THE ORIGIN OF THE SEASONS

HADES WAS LONELY. He wanted a wife but no-one was willing to share a life forever in the shadows. Even though he was a god, he could not take his place amid the clouds on Mount Olympus, but was forever destined to live deep below the earth, far away from the light of day and the fresh winds, the trees and the flowers — for he was the great Lord of the Underworld. The warmth of the sun never reached far below the earth and in his dark and dreary kingdom there were only the souls of the dead.

He would ride his huge chariot drawn by two coal-black horses up to the gates of the Underworld and look out at the sunlit fields. Sometimes he would visit his sister Demeter, goddess of the harvests, who lived in Sicily with her daughter Persephone. Demeter had golden hair, as gold as the fields of corn and the rich fruits in the orchards she made ripen. Demeter loved Persephone more than life itself and they would wander the fields of Sicily together, picking wild flowers and planting new seeds. As the years passed Persephone grew more beautiful than even her gentle mother, and Hades decided she was just the person to brighten up his gloomy underworld kingdom. But he knew Demeter would never agree to the marriage, so he plotted to carry Persephone away by force.

He waited until Persephone was wandering by herself one day. As she bent down to pick a clump of sweet-smelling violets, a huge chasm opened up

at her feet. And before she could escape, Hades appeared in his great chariot. He swept her up in his arms and turned the coal-black horses once more down deep under the earth. The chasm closed over and all was still and quiet as before, except for a few violets, crumpled and crushed on the grass.

In the evening Demeter came to look for Persephone. She had never stayed away from home for so long and in her heart Demeter knew that something dreadful had happened to her beloved daughter. She called and called her name, but only an empty echo came back. The next day Demeter looked further afield and the next and the next, but not a trace of Persephone did she find. She had vanished from the face of the earth.

In her great sorrow Demeter neglected her fields and trees. The corn withered on the stalk, the fruits shrivelled and died and famine walked the land. The flowers drooped and their brown petals fell to the ground, the leaves fluttered from the trees, dry and crumpled, and all the earth looked desolate.

Then Helios, the sun god, appeared one day as Demeter sat sadly looking out over the once-fertile land. What he told Demeter chilled the blood in her veins. Helios had seen Hades seize Persephone. Demeter knew her daughter would fade away to a shadow under the ground.

Then Zeus, great lord of all the gods, asked Iris, the rainbow goddess, to plead with Demeter to restore the fruitfulness of the earth, and to bring her back to Mount Olympus where she could be looked after. But Demeter refused to stay lest she miss an opportunity to save Persephone. Her greatest fear was that she would never see her daughter again, for she knew that if Persephone ate or drank anything while in the underworld she would not escape her dark prison. Anyone who tastes the food of Hades cannot ever leave that dark kingdom.

Then Zeus sent his winged messenger, Hermes, down to the underworld to demand the release of Persephone. Hermes shivered as he hastened down deep below the earth, he missed the warmth and light of the sun. Hades had just squeezed some juice from a pomegranate into Persephone's hands when Hermes landed softly by her side. She was seated before a huge table laden with food and Hades was doing his best to force her to eat. Hermes reached out just as she lifted her hand to her mouth to lick away the juice of the pomegranate. Six seeds fell to the ground but six she swallowed. Hades was triumphant! Now Persephone was his and would live by his side forever.

Hermes took pity on the weeping girl. He sped back to Zeus and told him what had happened.

Now Zeus was wise above all others and he thought for a long time before deciding what he should do. He knew that Demeter would never be happy again unless her daughter was restored to her, and if she was not happy she would continue to neglect the fields and forests. He knew that Hades was lonely and needed companionship and he knew that by eating the six seeds Persephone had unwittingly placed herself in his power. His decision was just and even handed. He decreed that Persephone must spend six months of every year with Hades in his underworld kingdom and she must respect him. The other six months of the year she could spend with her mother in the fields and meadows of Sicily.

And that is why for half the year the land is gloomy and the trees leafless. When Persephone goes down to her husband in the underworld, her mother grieves for her and neglects her duties. But Persephone keeps her side of the bargain. The underworld is a brighter place when she is there and even the great lord Hades is happy. Then in the spring, green shoots peep up out of the earth and Persephone returns to her mother. Flowers spring up wherever they walk together, fruit ripens on the trees and the corn turns golden in the sun.

HOW THE MOON CAME TO BE

A LONG TIME AGO, and perhaps even before then, there lived in the land of Guatemala a mighty chief and warrior who had a beautiful daughter. Because the chief did not want to share his daughter at all with anyone else, he hid her away where no-one else could see her or even speak to her. He was especially keen that the Sun should not look at her because he knew the Sun had ambitions.

Of course, once the Sun heard this (as he was bound to do), he determined that he would marry this beautiful girl. He did not give a fig for the chief's views on such a marriage, indeed he was very angry that the chief had been bold enough to think he might get away with hiding his daughter. And so the Sun plotted and planned and waited for his chance.

And his patience was rewarded. One day the chief went hunting in the forest, leaving his daughter behind with strict instructions that she should not leave the house and especially not speak to anyone. The Sun acted swiftly. He took up a huge turtle shell and hid behind it. As soon as the girl saw that the fierce heat had gone, she decided no harm could come if she went outside to sit in the shade. After all, she knew there was not another soul who would dare come near their house, so great was her father's power, and the heat made the house stifling. And so she slipped through the courtyard into the garden.

The Sun sneaked a quick look earthwards and nearly dropped the turtle shell in his excitement. The girl was indeed very beautiful. There was no time to lose. He sent a shaft of light down to earth, and bid the girl join him in the sky. She was tired of her solitary and lonely life, so without a backward glance she clambered up into the sky. The Sun received her most graciously and before long had persuaded her not only to stay, but to marry him then and there. And she was very happy with her new husband.

But what of her father down below on earth? He was purple with rage and had but one thing on his mind – revenge. It is one thing to swear revenge but quite another to achieve it, and against the Sun too. It took him many sleepless nights and angry days before he came up with a plan. He went to visit the best gunmaker in the whole of Guatemala.

'I wish you to make me a huge blowgun, the longest you have ever dreamed of,' demanded the chief. 'And I want you to make it sooner than yesterday!' He was terribly angry.

'I can certainly make you such a gun, but it is not the work of a few moments,' said the gunmaker. 'I will need to cut down the tallest bamboo, and remove all the pulp from inside and then polish it with rough bark and then...' But he was interrupted by the chief. 'I do not want to hear the ifs and buts – make me that blowgun by sunset. I wish to shoot the Sun who has run off with my daughter. So set to!' he ordered.

The gunmaker went away, shaking his head.

'Foolishness, foolishness,' he muttered quietly under his breath. 'Shooting the Sun indeed. Nothing wrong with a few tapirs or crocodiles, but the Sun? And what will he do with it when he has shot it?' But he valued his skin and so he set about making the biggest blowgun ever.

He collected ten strong men and they cut down a huge bamboo stalk which they dragged back to the village. The gunmaker then set all the women in the village to cleaning out the inside of the stalk and then to rubbing it down until it gleamed like gold. He ordered all the children in the village to collect clay from the river bed and to pile it up on great banana leaves spread out on the ground. Ten more men then rolled the clay into huge big balls, so big it took all ten men to lift just one.

Inside his great house the chief was taking mighty breaths and storing all the air in his lungs. It would take a lot of puff to blow one of the balls all the way to the Sun. As soon as the blowgun was ready, the gunmaker and the twenty strong men of the village dragged it, and the five huge clay balls, to the very top of the highest mountain. Then they scrambled back down to collect the chief so he didn't waste any of his breath climbing up himself.

Everyone was on tenterhooks. Would the chief manage to hit the Sun? And if he did what would happen to the Sun, and, much more importantly, what about the chief's beautiful daughter? The chief was twice his normal size with all the breath in his lungs as he put his lips to the blowgun. He gave a mighty puff and a clay ball sailed high into the sky, but not quite high enough.

The chief filled his lungs again to replace the air that he had used (although there was still plenty left as he had taken in huge gulps, and he was very angry). And with a mighty whoosh the second clay ball sped straight towards the Sun. This time it hit the Sun, but alas, it didn't knock the Sun out of the sky as the chief had wished. Instead his daughter, his beautiful daughter, tumbled towards the earth. She fell into the deepest ocean where she broke into hundreds of pieces.

All the pieces began to cry out loudly to be returned to the Sun. The darting silver fish in the sea were deeply distressed by her unhappiness — it was not her fault after all. They collected all the pieces and bound them back together again with their own scales and salt from the deepest ocean.

She was no longer a beautiful girl, but a glorious silver ball, shimmering and glittering in the water. Then the fish called on all the millions and millions of their kind in the sea and they formed themselves into a solid raft. With a mighty leap they soared out of the water and up, up into the sky.

But alas, they could not quite reach the Sun. They did manage to place the girl securely up in the sky however, and she gleamed down towards the earth through the darkness. She had become the Moon. The fish remained in the sky themselves, and you can still see them on a clear night as they twinkle in the Milky Way. The Moon circled round after the Sun endlessly, but she was never quite able to reach him. And so they follow each other to this day, the Sun glorious and bright and still ambitious, the Moon pale but glowing with the myriad silver scales the generous fish gave her, still hoping to catch up with her husband.

HOW MEN FIRST GOT FIRE

IN THE VERY BEGINNING, only Ka Kani had fire. He kept a firestick safely hidden from prying eyes in a hollow tree. Ka Kani and his wife and their children used the fire to keep warm in the cold desert nights, for it could be bitterly cold once the sun had set. And when they wanted to eat the antelope they had hunted, Ka Kani would first make a shallow hole in the ground and fill it with sticks and dried roots. Then he would place the firestick deep in amongst the dry kindling and before long a wisp of smoke would curl up into the still, piercingly blue sky.

One day, another bushman, Huwe, came to visit Ka Kani and his family. The ever hospitable Ka Kani invited Huwe to join in the evening meal. When Ka Kani's wife brought a huge platter of roasted antelope meat, Huwe was greatly puzzled. It looked like antelope meat and yet it was darker in colour than usual. And when he crammed a piece into his mouth he almost spat it out again in surprise. It was hot! It tasted quite different, too. It was succulent and juicy instead of being dry and stringy.

'Whatever am I eating?' asked the amazed Huwe. 'It looks like antelope, but I have never tasted anything so delicious in my life.'

And before he could stop them, Ka Kani's laughing children blurted out their father's greatest secret.

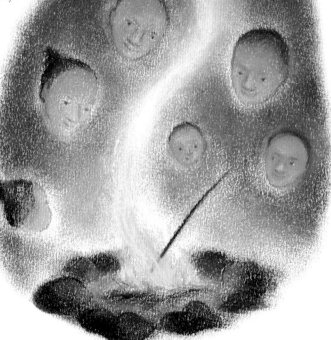

'Our mother puts the raw meat over the fire,' said the eldest boy. 'And then she turns it round and round until it turns brown and is all cooked,' added his sister. 'And that is why it tastes so good!' finished the smallest boy.

Now Huwe had not the slightest idea what the children were talking about, as he had never seen fire before. But he heard Ka Kani's sharp intake of breath, and he saw the frown that crossed Ka Kani's brow, so he understood very clearly that here was something he needed to investigate further. He did not wish to alert Ka Kani to his curiosity, so he just continued to eat the delicious meat with much smacking of lips and slurping of juice. And so Ka Kani let out his breath and smiled at his children before he walked with Huwe to the edge of the village.

But Huwe did not return home. He slept all night in a giant baobab tree and the next morning he crept back to Ka Kani's hut and hid himself carefully to watch all that went on. Ka Kani spent the day digging up roots and gathering fruit and nuts. As evening drew in, Huwe saw Ka Kani go to the hollow tree and take out what looked like a stick of wood, and yet it glowed strangely. Huwe crept a little closer. Ka Kani placed the strange stick in amongst a bundle of dried grasses in a hollow in the ground surrounded by some blackened stones, and then knelt down and blew gently under the grasses. To his astonishment Huwe saw a curl of smoke rise into the darkening sky. The grasses began to redden and then burst into flames.

As Huwe watched, Ka Kani placed a pot of water over the fire and then threaded some meat on a stick, which he also laid across the stones. A delicious smell wafted across towards Huwe. Soon the whole family had gathered around the fire and, warming their toes close to the embers of the fire, ate the delicious meat.

Huwe was angry. Why should only Ka Kani have the benefit of this wondrous thing? He waited until everyone was asleep and then he tiptoed cautiously over towards the hollow tree. He reached a searching hand into the trunk and drew out a handful of glowing firesticks. He broke them into a million pieces and threw them high, high into the sky. The firesticks rained down over the four corners of the earth and from that day forth men and women all over the world have been able to keep warm in the coldest of climates, and to cook and eat their food.

How Nanahuaztzin Became the Sun Goddess

FROM THE VERY BEGINNING OF TIME there had been four suns, one shining after the other, but the first was destroyed when jaguars ate the earth, the second by a hurricane. Then the third was consumed by a fiery rain and finally the fourth by an endless flood. The earth was dark.

As there was no light, nothing would grow, and the animals wandered around aimlessly. And so it was that the gods were looking for a fifth sun but; because they felt it was such a very great burden to shine constantly, they decreed that there should be two great lights over the world. One was to shine during the day, the Sun, and one during the night, the Moon.

The gods looked for two volunteers from their ranks, but who would willingly subject themselves to a never-ending future of merely shining in the sky? The gods were proud and arrogant and did not wish to give up any of their glory. Then a small voice was heard. It was Nanahuaztzin. She was a quiet creature, with a terrible disease that made her skin red and scaly. She was happy to think that she might be useful to the world, and so was ready to make this great sacrifice.

The gods muttered among themselves. Although they were relieved to have a volunteer, Nanahuaztzin was so pale and insignificant that surely she could not be

the one to light the world. It was agreed that she could be the Moon, who would only shine at night. When he saw the competition was the humble Nanahuaztzin, the boastful and vain Tecuciztecatl at once decided he would offer himself as the Sun. He thought he would surely be the winner and would shine gloriously forever.

Before the final selection ceremony, the two gods had to prepare themselves. They were required to build two great stone altars upon which the ceremonial fires would be lit. There they laid their offerings. On his altar, Tecuciztecatl piled up precious stones and sheets of the finest beaten gold, fine tools and jade figures of goats and eagles.

Nanahuaztzin had no such riches. She placed sweet-smelling fronds of orchids and honeycombs from the wild bees, and great sheaves of golden maize on her altar. The other gods sniggered behind their hands. Then Tecuciztecatl put on a great robe of gorgeously coloured feathers. Round his neck he clasped a golden amulet and on his head he settled a turquoise headdress. Nanahuaztzin wore a simple dress of the softest white llama wool. Round her neck she hung a chain of meadow flowers. The other gods laughed out loud.

As the stillness of deepest night settled over the mountain tops, huge fires were lit on each altar. The flames leapt high into the inky black sky, as if preparing the way for the blazing Sun. The laws decreed that whoever would be the Sun God had to leap into the heart of the fire and so be sacrificed to create the fifth sun. Tecuciztecatl was to go first. He felt his courage drain away, for now he had to show he was truly worthy to become the Sun God. He walked up to the altar, but when he felt the intense heat, he drew back and hesitated. Then he took another step forward, and swiftly several backwards. For a third time he tried, but again his courage failed him. The other gods were aghast at such cowardice and they jeered at Tecuciztecatl. He took another faltering step forward and stopped, the heat intense against his face. As he wavered, Nanahuaztzin calmly walked straight up into the fiery depth of her altar and disappeared. The gods roared their approval and, finally spurred on by such a display of quiet bravery, Tecuciztecatl stumbled into the fire burning on his altar.

But it was too late. A huge eagle dived into the heart of Nanahuaztzin's altar, then swept up into the heavens, a great flaming ball clasped between his fierce talons. The sky blazed with an intense golden light, and Nanahuaztzin shone over all the land, the huge, wonderful and warm Sun. The gods whooped and cheered, and all the animals on the earth welcomed the new Sun, and the plants turned their faces towards the light and warmth. Then the huge eagle swooped again, and this time between his talons crouched a pale wan thing. It was the Moon, the scared and trembling Tecuciztecatl. The eagle set the Moon in the sky to trail behind the fiery skirts of the magnificent Sun, and the gods mocked him in his shame. They tossed a rabbit up into his face, and to this day, if you look very carefully, you will see the rabbit's sad face in the full Moon as he pursues the Sun on her wonderful path across the sky.

HOW THE PEACOCK GOT HIS TAIL

ANY HARVEST MOONS AGO, the island kingdom of Lanka was the home of the god of treasure, Kuvera. Lanka's wealth was fabled throughout every kingdom. Glorious mansions of white marble were surrounded by endless gardens, filled with orchids and sweet-smelling frangipani trees. The island lay in the middle of a great ocean where it had been flung in a fury by Vayu, the god of the winds. The capital city of Lanka was enclosed by seven huge walls of gold and stone, and surrounded by seven deep moats filled with black fathomless water. But none of these defences were able to protect the city from the demon Ravana.

He was a truly terrifying sight. His huge body was as large as many mountains and covered in the scars of his many battles with the gods. He had ten heads and as soon as one was chopped off, another grew in its place as fast as a bolt of lightning. He had twenty great arms and with each one he brandished a mighty sword. His mouth gleamed with golden teeth. The god Brahma had been forced to grant this terrible demon one wish, and the wily demon had wished that no god or other demon could ever destroy him.

One day Ravana was chasing Indra, the Lord of the Rain and the Storm. Now Indra had bolts of lightning in his hand, but of course they were useless against the invincible Ravana, and so the only course open

to Indra was to hide. He looked around in desperation. The huge feet of Ravana were pounding the ground behind him and his hot breath was heavy on the air. Then, in front of the exhausted Indra there appeared a peacock. As quick as anything the peacock spread his tail and Indra crouched down underneath the soft feathers. The demon thundered by without even giving the small drab bird a second glance. Indra was safe for the moment.

He crawled out from under the peacock's tail and looked down at the bird in gratitude.

Peacocks were very plain birds in those days, no different from the modest little peahens. They were a dull brown colour with long, sweeping tails and very ugly feet. Indra stroked the peacock's head and a crescent of richly-coloured feathers sprouted on top of its head. Then Indra ran his fingers down the brown

feathers of its tail, and as he did so, the feathers turned to an iridescent green with thousands of golden eyes on each long plume. The peacock's body became plump and those feathers in turn became a brilliant blue. The peacock looked fabulous. The grateful Indra had made it the most beautiful bird in the world.

But alas the peacock became very vain. It strutted about, showing off its glorious tail at every opportunity. The little peahen bobbed about behind the silly creature, full of admiration for its beauty, but sad that it seemed to have forgotten all else in its vanity. Then the peacock looked down at its feet. Oh, but they were still wrinkled and ugly! The peacock gave a great shriek of horror and its glorious tail closed like a fan and sank to the ground. To temper his gift of glory Indra, the Lord of the Rain and the Storm, had given the peacock a harsh cry that was forever more to be a sign, people said, that bad weather was coming.

THE ORIGIN
OF THE WINDS

WHEN THE WORLD was very new, all was still and quiet in the vast cold northern lands. There were no trees and the snow fell in the endless darkness. There was no wind anywhere in the sky and the silence was very deep.

Near the mouth of a deep river there was a small collection of houses. The villagers were fishermen and hunters and during the long winter darkness they had time to sit and ponder as they huddled together for warmth.

One couple had been married for many seasons yet had no children, which was a great sadness to them. They worried about how they would manage when they grew old. There would be no-one to help them hunt and, when they died, no-one to mark their passing with a feast. Their sorrow began to gnaw at the wife.

Then one night she had a dream so vivid that she almost doubted she had been asleep at all. In her dream a fur-covered sled appeared out of the snow, driven by the Moon Spirit, Igaluk. The wife stepped in and the sled rose over the village and the river, as high as the glittering stars. On and on it sped through the endless dark until suddenly the sled swooped down and landed on a great sheet of ice, unbroken except for one small tree in the very middle. The Moon Spirit told the woman to make a doll out of the trunk of the tree and then all would be well with her and her husband, and indeed good fortune would spread all over the world. Just as the wife opened her mouth to ask a torrent of questions, she woke in her own bed, her husband by her side.

She was so convinced her dream had been real that she shook her husband awake immediately. Grumbling and muttering, he listened to her tale. And then she said he must go with all speed to find the place where the tree was growing so they could make the doll. The husband could see no point in making a wooden doll, but his wife fretted so that he took up his great axe and set off to look for the tree. The snow lay deep and no other footprint was to be seen, but as the husband plodded along, a strange path appeared in front of his feet. It glittered as bright as day, yet all around was deep darkness. Somehow he knew this path was there to guide his feet in the direction of the tree.

He walked for many hours, his eyes fixed on the shining path. And there was the great sheet of ice and, in the very middle, the small tree. It was so small he did not really need the great axe to cut it down, and he was able to place it deep in a pocket to carry it home. His wife was delighted to see him, and overjoyed when he carefully produced the small tree. That night the husband carved the trunk of the tree into a small boy, and from the branches he made a tiny spear, an axe and a knife. Then, with the chips of wood from his carving, he made a wooden bowl and a drinking mug. His wife made a tiny sealskin suit and a little pair of moccasins, and dressed the doll carefully. She filled the bowl and mug with food and water and set them in front of the doll. Then they went to bed.

In the morning, the food had been eaten and the water drunk. But the doll was nowhere to be seen. When the couple went outside they saw a line of tiny footprints leading to the edge of the village, but no further. The wooden doll had vanished.

Sadly the couple
went back indoors and closed the
door. Meanwhile the doll was striding along
the shining path the husband had taken the day
before. But the doll travelled even further. In fact he walked
until the sky met the icebound earth, where the walls are of ice and
the sky is midnight blue, pierced with millions of stars. The doll looked
up and there he saw the most curious thing. There in the deep blue of the
sky was a ragged patch, a patch made with seal skin, held at each corner by a
cord. It bulged slightly and there was a strange sound coming from behind the
patch, as if someone was blowing through their nose.

The doll took his tiny knife and cut one of the cords holding the
skin patch. All at once a swoosh of wind rushed through the gap in the
sky, and in the hurly burly of the wind there tumbled hundreds of
great birds, eagles and hawks, and all kinds of forest animals.
Once the birds and animals had all dropped through the skin,
the doll spoke quietly into the wind saying, 'East wind,
blow, blow as you will, sometimes gently,
sometimes fiercely and sometimes not at all.'
Then he covered the hole once more
and went on his way.

He walked down the shining path again and when he had gone as far south as possible, he found another patch in the sky. When he cut the cord this time, a soft, warm wind blew out, bringing with it flocks of brightly-coloured parrots, and mighty lions and tigers and all manner of jungle beasts. The doll spoke again. 'South wind, blow, blow as you will, sometimes gently, sometimes fiercely and sometimes not at all.' Then he covered the hole once more and went on his way.

This time he walked to the west and when he opened the patch in the sky, a great blustery wind threw a huge raft of silver fish and a mighty whale and flights of comical puffins through the gap. Again the doll spoke to the wind. 'West wind, blow, blow as you will, sometimes gently, sometimes fiercely and sometimes not at all.' Then he covered the hole once more and went on his way.

Now the doll walked to the cold north. Out from this patch in the sky came a bitter, icy wind and on its freezing breath came huge white bears and black-and-white penguins, and graceful white gannets. Ice and snow fell on the doll and he did not waste any time in closing the patch in the sky with his usual words, although this time he had to shout, so great was the howl of the wind. 'North wind, blow, blow as you will, sometimes gently, sometimes fiercely and sometimes not at all.' Then he went on his way, but this time he turned back to the village where the husband and wife sat sadly by their fire. They were delighted to see the doll and when he had told them all about his journey, they called the whole village together that they might know of the new winds that blew across the land.

So the little wooden doll did indeed bring good fortune as the Moon Spirit, Igaluk, had predicted. Never would mankind want for food, as the seas were teeming with silver fish, animals walked the land and birds filled the sky. And, of course, the four winds still blow across the whole world, sometimes gently, sometimes fiercely and sometimes not at all.

THE DRAGON OF CHAOS

IN THE BEGINNING, darkness lay over all the land and tumultuous waters roared in the great cracks in the earth. The very first beings in this dreary world were Apsu, who was the father and Lord of the Deep, and Tiamat, the mother and the Spirit of Chaos, who was a huge and terrible dragon.

Apsu controlled all the fresh water in the rivers, while Tiamat ruled over all the salt water in the seas. As the salt and fresh water came together, Apsu and Tiamat produced three children. Mummu, their first-born son, who was the Spirit of the Waves, and Lakhmu and Lakhamu, who were serpents. They in their turn produced two children, Anshar and Kishar, and then finally came the third generation – Anu, Ruler of the Sky, and Ea, the God of Wisdom. Now Anu and Ea were peacemakers and they loved order so they tried to organize the earth. But Apsu and Tiamat wanted to keep the darkness and chaos, so they decided to get rid of their troublesome great-grandchildren.

Tiamat called up all the terrible creatures from the deep seas to help her in her evil plan. As she watched from the stony shores of the great oceans, huge dragons with glittering scales, monster serpents with deadly poison running through their veins instead of blood, scorpion men and fish men, storm demons and wild dogs all stumbled on to dry land. As leader of this horrible troop, she placed an evil young god called Kingu. Anu and Ea went to try to make peace with Tiamat, but when they saw Kingu and Tiamat's dreadful army they fled in terror.

Ea had a brave and bold son, Marduk, and it was decided that he should face Tiamat and try to destroy her power. But first the gods decided to give him all the help they could. First they gave him the right to rule the universe so that no-one would question his authority. Then they gave him the mighty weapons of thunder and lightning. Anu gave him a magic net so he might trap Tiamat. This net was guarded at all four corners by the north and south, east and west winds so none could escape from beneath its folds. Finally, Marduk was given seven great winds to accompany him into battle — an evil wind, a tempest, a hurricane and a whirlwind, the fourfold and sevenfold winds and finally the wind that had no equal. Thus armed, Marduk rode into battle on his huge chariot pulled by four fierce and snorting horses, his thunderbolt in his hand, the winds whirling round his head.

Kingu fled at once, but Tiamat was made of sterner stuff. Deep in her cave, surrounded by her terrible sea creatures, she muttered curses and evil spells. Marduk taunted Tiamat to come out and fight him and, as he waited for her reply, he spread Anu's net across the mouth of the cave with the four winds at each corner. Then Tiamat roared out of the cave. She was an awesome sight. Fire belched from her slavering jaws, her huge wings flapped, glittering in the firelight, and sparks flew from her evil eyes. But she flew straight into the net, and no matter how she twisted and turned, she was firmly tied down. As she opened her mouth to bellow her rage, Marduk called up his evil wind to blow between her jaws

so she could not close them. Then all the other winds, the evil wind, the tempest, the hurricane and the whirlwind, the fourfold and sevenfold winds, and the wind that had no equal, poured into the dragon's body and she fell lifeless at Marduk's feet. When they saw that their mighty Tiamat was dead, all the other creatures fled back into the deepest oceans, where they no doubt lurk to this day.

Then Marduk split the body of the huge dragon into two parts. One he made into the heavens, and the other the earth. He made Anu Lord of Heaven and Ea Lord of the Deep. And he set the stars of the zodiac in their places and the moon high in the sky to measure the passing of the days and nights. Marduk then used his own blood mingled with clay from the earth to create human beings. Thus finally order was established out of chaos, chaos that was a huge and terrible dragon.

WHY THE MOON
HIDES HIS FACE

IN DREAMTIME, the time before all living memory, the ancestors created the shape of the land and the form of the people. They covered the land with trees and plants to feed the people, and laid down the customs and laws by which all future tribes would live. And when all was as the ancestors wished, they went back to sleep, but they left behind the song lines which are the doors to Dreamtime.

Then the Moon came down from the high sky and walked the earth with the animals and the people. He was an odd-looking creature. He was completely round with bright eyes and a permanent smile, but he had strange skinny arms and legs and he lumbered along like a great pale cheese. He was a sad being in spite of his smile – he was lonely and so he decided to look for a wife.

As he wandered from village to village, he soon became a laughing stock. Everyone knew he was after the prettiest girls, but they just laughed in his face. They had better suitors and anyway he was clumsy in his wooing. Before long, all the girls would hide if they heard he was coming so that when he stood in the centre of the village, the only people who were there to greet him were the old men. The Moon grew sadder and sadder.

One evening he wandered along a riverbank, singing softly to himself. Now whatever else was imperfect about the Moon, he did have the most beautiful voice and as he sang the stars bent down from the deep blue sky to listen to him. Also walking along the riverbank that evening were two young girls who did not know about the Moon's antics on earth. They heard the singing and they saw the stars bend towards the earth, and they wondered dreamily about the singer. Perhaps he was a great and mighty warrior? Perhaps he was a wild spirit from the skies? They decided to hide under a eucalyptus tree and wait for the singer to appear.

Their excitement grew as the wonderful voice drew nearer. But then, along the riverbank came such an odd-looking creature. He was completely round with bright eyes, but he had strange skinny arms and legs and he lumbered along like a great pale cheese. The girls were astonished, and deeply disappointed. Stifling their giggles, they ran to the river's edge where they had hidden their small boat, and jumped in, meaning to row home as fast as possible.

But the Moon had spotted them. He ran into the river, and pleaded to be taken up in the boat. The girls just laughed, but the Moon splashed into the water and tried to swim after them. How cold the water was, and how wet! The Moon spluttered and coughed and the girls realized he was in difficulty. They hauled him into the boat, full of remorse at their teasing but, as he recovered, he soon reverted to his old ways. He smiled at the girls and tried to kiss them, but they were not having any of it. In a second they tipped the Moon out of the boat again, and they watched as first the whole of his round shining face looked sadly up at them, then only half and then just a tiny crescent. Down, down he sank to the bottom of the river. The girls went home, scared and haunted, and they told no-one what had happened.

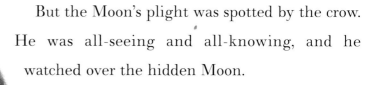

But the Moon's plight was spotted by the crow. He was all-seeing and all-knowing, and he watched over the hidden Moon.

The Moon spent three days at the bottom of the river and then he rose up and returned to the sky, where he sang softly to the stars and promised them that never again would he seek to wander the earth.

He was as good as his word. For three days he would hide his face completely and then he would slide into the sky, a thin shaft of light at first. Then he would grow bolder and reveal more of himself until the whole of his pale glowing face was shining over the land. But then he would remember his shame on earth, and gradually he would turn away again until there was only a crescent of silver showing and then nothing, until he smiled once again on the earth. To this day, the Moon hides his face from the earth for a while every month, and still the all-seeing and all-knowing crow watches over him.

THE FIRST SEVEN DAYS

I N THE VERY BEGINNING, God created heaven and earth. But the earth had no shape or form, it was flat and deeply dark. A bitter wind blew over the endless oceans and there was no single living thing to be seen. No people, no animals, no plants. As God moved across the water, he wanted to see his new land, so he created light. Suddenly everywhere was flooded with light, and God smiled. He decided there should be a time when brightness lit up everything, and this he called day. But there should also be a time when the earth was cloaked in darkness and this he called night. And so passed the first day.

On the second day, God made a wide blue sky. Then he filled it with white clouds which scudded across the vast blue expanse and God smiled. Then he made great black clouds, and rain fell from these clouds into the endless oceans. God did this so there would always be water on the land. And so passed the second day.

When the third day came, God gathered up the endless oceans and put them all in one place where they could whirl and swirl together. And where the oceans had been, he created land. He drew mountains out of the bare land and they rose high into the sky. He made deep valleys at the bottom of the huge mountains and then with a gentle breath he filled the valleys with green grass and herbs and vines and fruit trees. The air was filled with soft, sweet smells, and God smiled. And so passed the third day.

When the darkness rolled away again, it was the fourth day. God placed a hot orange ball spinning across the blue sky to warm the land, and he called it the sun. For the night, he created a pale shadowy ball which turned to lighten the darkness and this he called the moon. The sun and the moon would guide the passing of the year and the seasons forever more. Lastly, God flung a carpet of small sparkling lights into the inky darkness of the night, and these tiny points of light he called the stars. God smiled and so passed the fourth day.

It was the fifth day, the sun shone on the land and on the water and God decided to create some living creatures for the air and the sea. Deep in the oceans, he placed mighty whales and he gave them voices so they could sing to each other. He made the water glitter with shoals of silver-scaled fish and he made dancing seahorses and armour-plated lobsters. And God smiled at his glittering oceans. Then he looked high in the sky and with a glide of wings he created graceful gannets and shaggy black cormorants to skim over the water. He made a buzz of tiny hummingbirds and a clatter of gaudy parrots for the hot lands, and dark brooding eagles for the craggy mountains. He made sweet-singing nightingales and bright-eyed sparrows for the fields. God smiled at the tumbling feathers and so passed the fifth day.

Just before the sun came up, the birds began to sing and then it was the sixth day. Now God decided that the land needed creatures too, so he created great grey elephants with flapping ears, stripy tigers with noble heads. He made black-eyed pandas, rumbly brown bears and haughty camels. He made cows and sheep and horses who galloped for joy across the land. He made rootling pigs and secretive badgers, he made blundering moles and leaping frogs, he made tiny mice and dancing hares. And the air was filled with mooing and bellowing and roaring and trumpeting and squeaking. God smiled. Then he made a garden, the Garden of Eden. He filled it with spreading trees and perfumed flowers, lush grass and shady groves.

God needed someone to look after all the creatures and plants that he had created and so he breathed on the earth and created man and woman. He placed them in the Garden of Eden and told them to look after his wonderful creation. They would never want for food or shelter in the garden he promised, and he smiled at them. So passed the sixth day.

Thus did God create both heaven and earth and all that lived there, and when he looked down on the morning of the seventh day he smiled with pleasure. Then he rested and so passed the seventh day. Although all was wonderful in the world God had created, it did not last forever – but that is another story!

HEIMDALL'S JOURNEY

HEIMDALL WAS THE SENTRY at the gateway to the home of his fellow gods, Asgard. He guarded the great rainbow bridge, Bifrost, between Asgard and Midgard, the earth, with his mighty horn, Gjall, in his hands. If danger threatened the gods, he would wind his horn and its blast would echo the hills around. His eyesight was so keen he could see a bird sitting on its nest hundreds of giant paces away, and his hearing so acute he could hear the wool growing on a sheep. Midgard had been created from the dying body of the giant, Ymir, who was slain by Odin, the god of battle and death and greatest of all. Ymir's body made the earth, his bones the mountains and his blood the rivers and seas.

It was spring, and Heimdall walked over Bifrost and into Midgard. He left Gjall behind and walked in disguise so none might know he was a powerful god. He walked all day and all night and another day. As dusk fell, his feet took him towards a simple shelter huddled up against a rock face. He flung back the hide over the entrance and found himself looking at Ai and Edda, descendants of Ask, the first man in Midgard, who was created from an ash tree, and Embla, the first woman, who was created from an elm.

Ai was suspicious of their unexpected visitor and demanded to know his name. Heimdall said he was called Rig and so he was allowed over the threshold. Edda gave him a bowl of soup and her place by the fire, and soon the god had stretched out his long legs and was quite at home.

Heimdall spoke gently and beguilingly, and Ai and Edda were quite won over by their mysterious guest. The shelter was dirty and smoky, but Heimdall stayed for three nights, sharing the rough bed of sacking by the fireside. And then he departed, as the last snows melted from the mountain tops, thanking Ai and Edda for their hospitality.

Now nine months later, Edda gave birth to a son. And oh, he was an ugly creature! But he grew to be strong and he worked hard and long for Ai and Edda, who called him Thrall.

When Thrall was a young man, a woman appeared one day by the hide door of the shelter. She was as rough and ready as Thrall and so they liked the look of each other. Her name was Thir and before long she and Thrall were married, and they produced a great brood of children, ugly but strong boys and coarse but hard-working girls. From these children and their children and their children came the race of thralls, or slaves.

Meanwhile, Heimdall had continued his journey. He walked and walked until he came to a farmhouse, well kept and tidy. Heimdall knocked at the door and walked in. There sat Afi and Amma. They were busy, she with her spinning wheel, he carving with his sharp knife. They were startled to see Heimdall standing in front of their fire and Afi asked their unexpected guest to explain himself. Heimdall said his name was Rig and that he sought shelter for the night. Afi and Amma made him welcome and when it was time to eat, Amma produced bread and cheese and a tankard of beer. Heimdall spoke gently and beguilingly, and Afi and Amma were soon at ease with their mysterious guest. When it was time to sleep, Heimdall once more shared a bed with his hosts, and so he stayed with them for three nights. And then, as the sun rose over the mountains,

Heimdall thanked Afi and Amma for their hospitality and departed.

Now nine months later Amma gave birth to a son. He was a bright, sunny child with quick ways and skilful hands, and they called him Karl. As he grew up he learned how to plough and how to build a barn and he was very useful to Afi and Amma on the farm.

When Karl was of a marriageable age, Afi and Amma found him a wife. Her name was Snör. She was bright and pretty and she made a good home for Karl. They had many children, craftsmen for sons and home-makers for daughters, and from these children and their children and their children came the race of peasants.

Still Heimdall walked the length and breadth of Midgard. This time his way took him to a fine hall. Fields of well-tended crops surrounded the great wooden posts that marked the boundaries, and the rooms inside were light and airy. Heimdall walked in through the wide doors and there he found Fathir and Mothir. Fathir was making a new bow for himself with many feathered and sharpened arrows, and Mothir sat by his side. She was elegant and dressed in a fine woollen robe of the deepest blue, and her pale blonde hair was wound in plaits about her head. On her lap lay a piece of embroidery.

Fathir rose to his feet courteously, wondering all the while why his servants had not announced their visitor. Heimdall inclined his head and explained he wished only shelter for the night. When Fathir asked his name, the god said it was Rig. Mothir rose to offer their unexpected guest a seat by the fire, and Heimdall was soon at his ease, talking to Fathir about his new bow. Mothir summoned her servants and a great feast was soon set out. There were fine linen napkins

and the bowls were chased with silver. There was wine to drink and soft bread, roasted fowl and great round cheeses. They ate and drank well, and long into the night. Heimdall spoke gently and beguilingly and once again he found himself sharing a bed with his hosts, this time a huge carved wooden bed with many furs and rugs to keep out the night chills. And so he stayed for three nights. Then he departed, thanking his hosts for their hospitality.

Now nine months later, Mothir gave birth to a fine son. He had gleaming golden hair and a wise look in his eyes. Fathir and Mothir called him Jarl and he grew to be a noble man like his father. He learnt to shoot with a bow and to ride a horse as fast as the winds. He could swim like a fish and he wielded a sword like a warrior.

Suddenly Heimdall appeared again one day, and took Jarl into the forest. There he opened his hand and showed Jarl the magic runes. All day long, Heimdall taught Jarl about the secret meanings that lay within the runes. And then he revealed that he was Jarl's father and that he was a king and so would Jarl be a king after him. Jarl's heart soared.

He realized that he had always felt different from his fellow beings. He left Fathir and Mothir and built his own hall, and when he was ready he sought Erna, the daughter of a chieftain, for his wife. In time they had many children, and to the first born Jarl explained the secrets of the runes. From this son and his sons and his sons came the race of kings.

Heimdall returned home. He crossed the rainbow bridge and entered Asgard once more. And so it was that Heimdall created the races of man.

INDEX

BIBLIOGRAPHY

American Indian Myths and Legends Richard Erdoes, Alfonso Ortiz (Pimlico, 1997)

The Enchanted Orchard Dorothy Sharp Carter (Harcourt Brace Jovanovich, 1973)

The Stories of Vanishing Peoples John Mercer (Allison and Busby, 1982)

Myths and Legends of Many Lands Evelyn Smith (Thomas Nelson, 1936)

The Book of Origins (Ernest Benn, 1979)

Myths and Legends From Around the World Sandy Shepherd (Evans, 1994)

Gods Men and Monsters Michael Gibson (Peter Lowe, 1977)

History of Myths Retold Diana Ferguson (Chancellor Press, 2000)

The Greek Myths Robert Graves (Penguin, 1992)

Spirits Heroes and Hunters Marion Wood (Peter Lowe, 1981)

The Kingfisher Book of Mythology (Kingfisher, 2001)

History of Mythology Veronica Ions (Chancellor Press, 2002)

Early China Wendy Boase (Hamish Hamilton, 1977)

A Companion to World Mythology Richard Barber (Kestrel Books, 1979)

The King James Bible (Eyre and Spottiswoode)

The Bible Designed to be Read as Literature (William Heinemann)

The New English Bible (Oxford University Press/Cambridge University Press)